The Darkest Ocean

Her heart is an ocean of secrets...

KAREN WEAVER

Copyright © 2019 Karen Weaver

First published in Australia in 2019
by MMH Press
www.mmhpress.com

All rights reserved. No part of this book may be used or reproduced by any means, graphic, electronic, or mechanical, including photocopying, recording, taping or by any information storage retrieval system without the written permission of the copyright owner except in the case of brief quotations embodied in critical articles and reviews.

The author and publisher have made every effort to contact copyright holders for material used in this book. Any person or organization that may have been overlooked should contact the publisher.
National Library of Australia Cataloguing-in-Publication data:
The Darkest Ocean/ Karen Weaver
Fiction/ Women's Fiction.
Editor: Teena Raffa-Mulligan
Cover design: Everly Yours Cover Design

ISBN: 978-0-6486645-0-5 (sc)

This book is dedicated to my readers.
Thank you. x

'I'm just not ready, Jase.'

He's not listening to me. I don't know how many times I have to tell him. We stand on the street outside the small beachside restaurant where his parents got engaged thirty years earlier, where he's invited all our family and friends along to witness his after-dinner proposal. What was he thinking? What are they thinking this minute? For of course I've turned him down. They won't understand it. He certainly doesn't so I tell him again, 'I'm not ready.'

He shakes his head. 'I'm beginning to think you never will be. It's been six years, Áine.'

'You shouldn't have sprung it on me. You know I don't like surprises.'

'It can't have been that much of a surprise after all this time. It's not as if we haven't spoken about it. I thought you loved me.'

'Of course I loved you.'

That came out wrong. I can tell by his face, so I quickly amend it. 'I do love you, Jase, but I'm not ready to get married, not yet.'

'Why don't we take a walk by the beach?' he says, reaching for my hand.

Usually that would make me feel safe. Not tonight, though, so I snatch my hand back and snap, 'I need some space,' then head off along the street without a backward glance.

He doesn't get the message and I hear his footsteps hurrying after me.

'Áine,' he calls.

With a sigh, I stop. 'What?'

'I'm not letting you walk around the streets in the dark on your own. I'm coming with you.'

'Suit yourself.' I shrug and march off towards the beach.

When I reach the foreshore, I kick off my shoes and walk across the cool sand to the water's edge. It's dark yet the full moon illuminates the water, creating an illusion of lightness. This place has always been a sanctuary for me, somewhere I feel connected to something deep, but it's also something that holds me back from embracing the life he is offering.

What is wrong with me? Jase is everything I could ever hope for in a life partner and yet I can't commit. I can't tell him why and I can't expect him to wait until I'm ready. If I ever will be. It's not fair to keep him hanging on like this. I don't want to let him go but I have no choice. I have to set him free. The pain of his broken heart now will be less of a burden than the alternative if I stay.

He reaches my side and without looking at him, I admit, 'We do need to talk.'

'You're not going to tell me what I want to hear, are you?' There is pain in his voice.

'I'm sorry. I can't explain but I have to go away. There is something I need to work out.'

'You don't need to do that. Whatever it is, we can work it out together and when you're ready...'

'Jase, I need to go.'

He crushes me against his chest as if he will never let me go and I feel like I can't breathe. At last he releases me and holds me away from him, his eyes searching mine. He doesn't need to ask if I will change my mind. He knows I won't.

As I watch Jase walk slowly away with his head bowed, I feel nothing. I am completely disconnected from my emotions. But I know what I need to do. I need to go home, I need to face the secrets of my past. Perhaps then I will allow myself to commit to life.

* * *

Three days later I am at the airport when my phone rings. It's my sister, Cass. She's been on my case since I turned Jase down, can't understand why I wouldn't jump at the chance to marry one of the most eligible bachelors in town.

'Where are you?' she asks. 'Jase is here, he wants to talk to you.'

'Tell him I can't right now. I'm at the airport about to board a plane to Dublin.'

'Dublin!' she shrieks. 'Áine, do not get on that plane.'

'I have to, Cass.'

'I'm putting Jase on the phone...'

I should hang up but I don't.

'Áine, please don't go,' he begs. 'I need you to stay.'

'I can't. If I go and do what I need to do it will be better for us. It's the only way I will be able to love you the way you deserve to be loved.'

'I'll come with you. Please don't go on your own. I love you.'

'I know.' I end the call before he hears the sob I can't hold back.

* * *

When I arrive in Dublin, Mammy and my brother Donal are waiting for me at the airport.

'Cass called then?' I say.

'She messaged your brother on Facebook. You know she doesn't talk to me. She's worried about you.'

'I just needed to come home for a bit.'

Mammy gives me a hug. 'When you're ready let me know, love, and we can chat about whatever it is.'

I am suddenly transported back to my childhood self where a cup of tea and a chat with Mammy put everything right again. Well, almost everything…

Donal takes my bag and we go to the car. I catch up on all the news during the drive to our family home where little seems to have changed since I left 10 years ago.

'Your room is ready for you, love,' says Mammy and makes her way to the kitchen to put on the kettle. 'Donal, light the fire, love, it's bitter cold in here,' she adds.

Entering my room is like going back in time. Nothing has changed. My white dressing table and stool are waiting to invite me to play make up, my big bed still has a fluffy duck feather pillow and duvet cover covered in grey and pink zig zag stripes because that was all the range back then. I sit on the bed and breathe in the familiar smells. It feels good to be home, good to know that Mammy is close by. I'm being given the opportunity to press reset and start again. I have much to think about. Every action causes a reaction but if I'm going to move forward with my life, I must break the silence. That's easier said than done.

That night I can't sleep. Flashbacks shatter all my hopes of a peaceful night's rest. Living in Australia I slept well, perhaps because I had left the hurt behind in Ireland, buried it deep. But realising the residue of my past was holding me back from a happy future compelled me to take action, regain my power. My psychologist has told me true healing can occur when we have the strength to face our demons and release them for good. I've chosen to be brave though I have had to fly from one side of the globe to the other to do so.

Something has awoken inside me, something that has been asleep for too long. Something I kept tucked away inside, but that festers inside of me and breaks my heart. Those who have wronged me only hold the power I allow them to have. I can't truly be free until I face the person who stole my childhood.

I begin the day with a shower and in many ways it cleanses me from the thoughts and emotions that disturbed my night. Refreshed, I go to the kitchen, where Mammy is bustling about.

She has put the kettle on. 'Morning, love. Tea and toast?'

'Yes, please.'

As I fetch cup and plates, I know she is waiting for the right moment to ask me why I have suddenly returned home without warning so I say quietly, 'I need to process what happened, Mam, it's time.'

The blood drains from her face and her hand trembles as she pours the tea. 'Would ye not be better leaving those ghosts to rest?'

'I can't, Mammy, they're not resting inside of me and are stopping me from moving on with my life.'

'Then whatever will be will be and I will support ye no matter what happens.'

It is all I needed to hear. I hug her so tight, tears of relief streaming down my face. Tears that should have been shed a long time ago.

'Aw, love, just let it out,' she murmurs, patting my back. 'It doesn't do any good letting it fester inside.'

'No,' I say through my tears.

She pushes me back to listen to her.

'Áine, love, at some point I need to know what really happened. I'm stronger than you think. And now that your dad is not around dictating things without my blessing I want to help you with your healing because I wasn't there for you at the time as I should have been.'

'Thanks, Ma. That means a lot. I will tell you, just not right now.'

'Of course, love.'

She hugs me tighter. I know she doesn't want to let go. She wants to hold me and protect me and if she could, I know she would go back in time and see the signs more clearly.

I whisper, 'It wasn't your fault, Ma, you were not to know.'

Tears are running down her cheeks too and it shocks me. I've never seen her cry before. She grabs a bunch of tissues and mops at her eyes, then takes a deep breath and gives me a smile that touches my heart.

'I'm so proud of you, love. Now let's have that cup of tea. We'll get you through this so that you can go marry that lad of yours.'

***

Boarding the visitor bus at McCullin Jail numbs me but as we draw closer to the gates after what feels like one of the longest journeys I've ever taken, all kinds of emotions begin to ripple through me. Desperately I try to block them before they take hold.

The bus stops, the doors open and I am the last to get off. The visitor check-in process is invasive, as if we too are criminals but I understand the reason. It is one more thing to endure before I take this step towards healing.

At last I enter the meeting room and scan the waiting inmates for the person I have come to visit. I can't see him, or at least recognise him and have to ask a guard.

I am directed to an old man with a long grey beard, dull duck-egg blue overalls and a distance in his eyes. I walk across and he stares at me with unrecognising eyes. I am about to walk away when he says, 'Áine, is that you?'

The sound of his voice pulsates through me. Bile rises in my throat but I swallow it down. I pull my shoulders back to show my strength.

'Yes, it is.'

'What are you doing here?'

My blood begins to boil and I have to take a hold of my emotions again.

He attempts to leave the table but there is no way I am going to let that happen.

I swallow all of the fear that consumes me and sit down. 'I need to talk to you.'

He is now the one filled with fear. He sits back down.

There is a deep discomfort in me as I sit across the table from a man who was instrumental in stealing my innocence but I hold my power so that he is the uncomfortable one.

'Why me?' I ask. 'Why did you choose me? I looked up to you, I loved you and you took advantage of that.'

'You were giving me all of the signs.'

'I was fourteen years old, you are my uncle. You were supposed to protect me from evil.'

He looks confused. 'You don't understand.'

'Help me understand.'

I stare him down, wait precious minutes for an answer. An answer that will help me to move on with my life. *I am not leaving without the truth.*

After what seems an interminable silence he sags back in his chair. 'Okay, okay, I will tell you.'

I relax slightly. I didn't realise how tense my shoulders were.

'I'm not your uncle. Did you ever see me in your house?'

The question catches me off guard and I frown. 'No. I don't think you were at any of our family occasions.'

'I wasn't.' He moistens his lips. 'Your father and I had a deal. Your mother thought we were business partners and in a way we were. I bought you from your dad when you were about four. The deal was that he would bring you around regularly so that we could become acquainted and when you were sixteen he'd hand you over to me for good. But you grew up so fast, and my attraction for you became stronger.'

I recoil and gag, remembering the uncomfortable cuddles he gave me when I was left with him. But he always seemed to have restraint, well until…

'I paid a lot for you, I was a wealthy man you know. And now your father is the wealthy one.'

'My dad died last year.'

'Oh, I didn't realise, well I would say I'm sorry but I'm not…'

'Yes fine, now get to the point.' I'm holding my nerve and it's getting harder.

'We brought your handover forward two years and you and I were to disappear to another country. A country where it is not such a foreign concept for an older man to marry a young woman. And all was going well until you took off.'

'You raped me!'

'No, you were to become my wife, you were mine to have.'

'You raped me!' I repeat. He *must* understand.

He no longer defends his words. 'The deal was broken when you took off and your father wouldn't return the money. Instead, when they found you they brought you to a local police station and well, you know the rest, here I am paying for something that was a deal. Do you know what they do to so-called child molesters in here?'

I don't respond, I refuse to feel any empathy for the man who stole my innocence.

'I heard you were pregnant, what happened to my child?'

'I wasn't pregnant.'

'Well, I heard differently. Shipped off to Australia, you were.'

I choose to end the conversation. I have heard what I needed to hear. He shouts after me but I cannot listen to one more word from this man, he repulses me. I am glad he is behind bars, I wouldn't want someone else to suffer because of his sick desires.

As I leave the guard asks, 'Is everything okay, love?'

'It will be,' I answer.

* * *

The ocean is calling so I must go. It's a different call than before. I didn't mean to drown the last time. I was not myself, the demons of what I had just been through consumed me and I could not see a future without severe pain consuming my every thought and emotion. But for some reason that day, I escaped a future that would have broken me beyond repair.

I stand in the place physically but not emotionally. A missing piece of the puzzle has slotted into place. I now understand why I never felt comfortable in my own home, in my own identity. My father, who should have loved me unconditionally and protected me, betrayed me. And yet through the knowledge of that betrayal I may have found freedom.

The sun sets on the horizon and with it I feel a new dawning enter my soul. It will take time to fully process everything, but I now have a new life pulsating through me, a zest I haven't felt in some time.

My phone rings. It's Ma.

'Áine, love, thank goodness, where are you?'

'I'm down at Dockman's Beach.'

'Oh love, wait there, don't do anything stupid, I'm coming to get you.' There's an urgency in her voice.

I tell her I'm okay, not to worry, I'm just releasing some of the hurt from the past and I'll be home soon.

It doesn't reassure her. She insists on coming to get me anyway.

***

On the way home Ma asks about my day. 'Did you get the answer you were searching for?'

'Yes and no.'

'My love, if I can help, you need to let me know.'

I give her a bright smile. 'I'm much stronger than you think I am.'

'I know, love, but I am your Mammy and it is my job to worry about you and help you when I can.'

'It wasn't easy visiting him,' I admit, 'but it was exactly what I needed to do.'

'Maybe one day you'll share it all with me.'

'I will when it's time, Mam,' I promise. Though it may never be the full story. The shame would kill her if she knew the truth about my father. 'For now let's just go home and spend some time together before I fly back.'

'You're flying back already?'

'Yes, tomorrow if I can get a seat on a flight. There's something I must do.'

And it can't wait. The urgency to get back to see Jasei building. I hope with all my heart that I haven't ruined things with him. There is so much I want to tell him; the depth of my love and the dreams I have of the life we will build together. I can't do that over the phone. For the first time in my life I have hope, real hope. I am letting love in and trusting someone else to share my life. I am beginning to feel worthy of what Jase has to offer me.

Next morning I jump out of bed with a zest for the day I have never felt before. It doesn't take long to pack as I hadn't really unpacked, then I join Mammy in the kitchen.

She leans on the breakfast bar to face me. 'What is it love?'

Tears well in my eyes. 'I'm finally ready to love Jase and it's a great feeling. I never thought I would feel like this and it's so good, so good I cannot even begin to tell you, but...'

'Ah the "but". What is it love, what's holding you back?'

'I'm going have to share all of my secrets with him, he needs to know the real me, but what if he can't handle it and rejects me?'

She takes both of my hands in hers and looks me right in the eyes. 'Sure, love, is it not better to be loved for who you are rather than who you're not? That's true love.'

She's right. If he truly loves me, he will love me warts and all.

'He sounds like a very special lad.'

'He is ma, very special.'

She reaches up and touches my cheek. 'Then you have nothing to worry about.'

I hope and pray she's right.

'Ma, why do you and Cass not get on?'

Pain flashes through her eyes. 'Cass was always Daddy's little girl. I loved her from the moment I laid eyes on her but she only had eyes for your dad. She even refused my milk when she was born, she only wanted your dad to feed her. Can you imagine, your firstborn rejecting you! It was tough but I knew I could be her mum from afar. Even when your dad went to work she was unsettled all day until he came home, and he...well, he wanted to keep her all to himself. He poisoned her beautiful mind against me. She pauses and traces the rim of her tea cup with one finger.

'One day when she was sixteen she came barging into the house, packed her bags and ran out the front door. I tried to find out what was wrong but she wouldn't talk to me. What I found strange is that she refused to talk to your dad too. She didn't come back home but I had some of my friends from church keep me informed of her wellbeing and it helped my aching heart to know that she was okay.'

There's a long silence so I prompt her: 'And?'

'Well, your father never spoke of her, it was if she no longer existed. She did come back to the house to say goodbye just before she moved to Australia and that day she actually gave me a hug, but no words.' Mammy shakes her head sadly. 'I felt pain in her heart, I wanted to help her heal it but she was set on moving away. I thought a new start would do her the world of good.'

'Mammy, she has a beautiful life in Australia.'

'Yes, I see that, Donal shows me some things on Facebook.' A single tear trickles from her eye. 'I would love to meet my grandchild, Áine.'

'You will.'

'When I saw Cass had the same pain as you, I knew you needed to be with her. There was something I couldn't protect you from here and you needed a new start too.'

A sense of clarity washes over me. I hope I'm wrong and yet it's as if nother piece of the puzzle has slotted into place.

'You did good, Mammy. Look at me, I'm doing good.'

Lifting the palm of her hand to cup my face, she beams with pride. 'I know, look at you, so in love and ready to build a life with the man of your dreams.'

'I am, aren't I?'

'You are, my love.'

There's a knock at the door. Given we are situated miles from town, this seldom occurs. Mammy answers the door and I hear a familiar voice.

'Jase! Is that you?' I dash straight into his arms and give him the biggest kiss.

'Hey, babe, what a hello. That was worth the trip in itself.'

The Darkest Ocean

Mammy is smiling fit to burst. 'Welcome, welcome,' she says.

We gather in the kitchen and I tell Jase I was rushing to get back to him. It is so good to see Mam and Jase getting along. My heart feels fuller right now than it ever has. We spend the evening with my Mammy, I know how much it means to her that we are there and I can talk to Jase later. We sit in the warm cosy living room with the open fire blazing and talk about everything and nothing. Donal drops in for dinner and is shocked to see that Mammy doesn't have anything ready, so he offers to go get us all a Chinese takeaway. Eventually Mammy reluctantly retreats to bed as her eyes won't stay open for another moment and before midnight and Jase and I do too. That night is special. We lie in each other's arms and I know there is nowhere else I want to be. I feel safe and that Jase would never do anything to hurt me. He is the love of my life and I know I am his. Together we are whole. That night is magical.

It is not the time to tell him my secrets. That can wait for tomorrow.

***

We arrive at the ocean's edge. Mammy packed us a picnic and so we set it up. It is a beautiful day and there are lots of other people around.
I never want to lose or change what we have right in this moment but I must tell Jase. I must!
Taking a deep breath, I reach for his hand. 'Jase, I have to tell you something.'

'Sure.' There is concern in his eyes as he gives me his full attention.

'I feel that I must tell you my secrets, the secrets that have held me back from loving you with all of my heart.'

'I love you no matter what, Áine,' he says and I know he means it.

But will he feel the same when he knows the truth about me? Anxiety knots my stomach and makes my heart race. Only the love in Jase's eyes gives me the strength to continue.

'Ten years ago, I came to this beach in despair. I had been through a traumatic experience and I wasn't thinking straight.' My breath hitches but I have to say it. 'Jase, I was raped.'

He pulls me close, his heart beating so hard in his chest that I can feel it. He strokes my hair and his voice is thick with emotion as he says, 'Oh no, oh my precious one. What monster would do that to you?'

'It's a long story.' I sigh against his chest. 'Even I didn't know it all till now. That's why I came back here. I needed answers, needed to know, why me? I had to confront him, the man who almost destroyed my life.'

'I want to kill him.' Jase's fists clench and unclench. 'And I would for you.'

'I know you would. But it wouldn't change anything. What's important is that I move forward. And now, I finally feel that I can. But I was so worried that when I told you about my past, you'd see me differently.'

'I do. I see your strength and your resilience. And now I understand why you held back, why you couldn't love me completely. If only you'd told me sooner, I would have been there for you.'

'I was afraid I'd lose you, once you knew. And Jase...there's more.'

'Nothing you say will change the way I feel about you. So, sweetheart, tell me.'

'I was in a bad place, for months after it happened. I couldn't think straight. I was given tablets to help me but they didn't. One day I came here to this beach and I wanted to feel free, free of the overwhelming feelings. I remember standing here, at the edge of the ocean and it called me, it called so loud! I felt compelled to answer the call so I ran into the bitter cold water and I swam. I swam and I swam. When I was a way off shore I let myself sink.

'I remember the feeling of lightness, of no noise in my mind anymore. The only sensation was peace. I floated under the water for a time, I didn't want the peacefulness to ever stop, but of course I needed air, I needed air really badly. The surface seemed a long way away. I began to blank out and could feel myself sinking further and then...nothing.

Suddenly a shock pierced through my body, my eyes jolted open and there it was, a glowing light. I thought I had died and the light was calling me so I followed it. My urge to breathe was not my main focus and yet I needed to breathe so badly. My focus cleared and I saw the light was in fact a glowing jellyfish. It was guiding me to the surface, it must have stung me, shocking my body and mind to react and come alive again.

'The next thing I knew, an arm grabbed me and pulled me to the surface where I spluttered and choked and caught my breath. I tried to see who had saved me but my vision blurred and I must have passed out, for the next thing I knew I woke up in a hospital bed, my mammy by my side.'

'And you never found out who saved you?'
'No.'
'Pity.'
'Yes.'
'And that's it?'
'Not quite...I was pregnant but the incident caused a miscarriage. Then, too, there was the trauma of the whole story of my rape coming out and the rapist being charged and it was in all the newspapers and on the TV. Fortunately he pleaded guilty, so that did make things a lot easier for me than they could have been. But it felt like I was living a nightmare.'

'A few weeks later Cass called to ask if I wanted to come see her in Australia and she would take care of me. I was young and confused but Mammy thought it would be good for me to have some time away, a little holiday to make me feel better, so I went.

'We soon discovered I was still pregnant. I must have been having twins and lost only the one after I nearly drowned.'

'You have a child?' asked Jase.

'Yes...and no. Cass had been trying for a baby for years and had recently miscarried. She begged me to give her my baby. I owed her so much, Jase, she had taken such good care of me and what sort of life could I give a child? So I agreed. But when I held him in my arms I didn't want to let him go. I'd never felt anything as strong as the heart connection I felt in that moment.

'Cass knew, she saw it, and reminded me of my promise. I handed my baby boy over though my heart was breaking. My sister changed from that day. Of course she was afraid to lose him. She insisted the only way it would work was for me to be his auntie and threatened to send me straight back to Ireland if I crossed any boundaries. There was no way I was going to leave his side, so I went along with it.'

'Damien is your son?'

'He is. But he must never know the truth, it would shatter his world. Promise me you won't say a word about what I've told you. Ever.'

'My lips are sealed. Oh, my darling, you've been through such heartache. It explains so much.'

He stands up and pulls me to my feet, then gets down on one knee there on the seashore and pulls out the small velvet box he pulled out a week ago. I know what's coming and tears of joy fill my eyes.

'Áine O'Toole, I promise to love you forever. I promise to make you feel safe and loved for the rest of our lives together. Áine, will you marry me?'

My heart wants to burst with happiness. 'Yes, I will, of course I will.'

He places the ring on my finger and it is perfect. I turn it this way and that and it shimmers in the moonlight. I can't quite believe this is happening.

'You still love me even though you know?'

'I love you more because I know.'

Words elude me. We stand wrapped in each other's arms on the beach for what feels like an eternity, listening to the waves lapping the shore, feeling the gentle embrace of the night breeze.

Then I realise we are not alone.

'Mum? What are you doing here?'

'I was worried about you. Did I see what I think I saw?'

I hold out my hand and show her my ring.

She beams with joy and hugs me close. 'To think that ten years ago today I was pulling you out of this ocean not knowing if you were to live another day. Now here you are, you've built an amazing life for yourself and found the love of your life. I...'

'You saved me?'

'Yes, love. I knew something was wrong when you left that day so I followed you. But that's in the past. I can rest now, I don't need to follow you to the darkest ocean anymore, my beautiful Áine. Let's go home.'

Yes, I am free of the darkness but as we pack up and follow her up the beach to the car park I realise I will have to find a way to tell her about Damien.

***

Getting ready to leave Ireland is bitter sweet. Living so far away from my mum makes saying goodbye hard and she's not getting any younger.

'Are you okay, my beautiful fiancé?'

'I like the sound of that.'

Jase playfully swoops me up in his arms and kisses me.

The feeling of happiness and sadness fuses together and he senses the change of mood.

Concern furrows his brow. 'What's wrong? You're not having second thoughts...'

'No.' I look at my ring and smile. 'I'm just sad to leave Mum is all, we have really connected the past few days and I will miss her. I will miss her not being in my life, a granny to our children when we have them. It was different when Dad was around but I see Mum for herself now and I will really miss her.'

'Would she come to Australia?'

'I never thought of asking her.'

'Well, why don't you ask her and then we can make it happen.'

I feel like the luckiest woman in the world, I am no longer out there battling life on my own, I have a partner who loves me unconditionally. Some people search their whole lives and never find what I have right here by my side. 'I can't wait to marry you,' I tell my lovely man.

'Then let's not wait, let's set a date now.'

'So should I be going hat shopping?' asks Mum five minutes later when I break the news.

'Yes, Mammy. But there is one thing…we're getting married in Australia. Will you come? We'll pay your way of course. And you can stay with us.'

Happiness ripples through every part of me when she says nothing would keep her away, though I can't help but notice there is a hint of sadness in her smile.

'You're worried about Cass, aren't you?'

Mammy nods. 'Just a little, it's been so long and she didn't come back for your dad's funeral.'

'It might be a good opportunity for you to clear the air.'

'You're right, love. And to go to Australia! Sure, I've never left Ireland before and now I'm going to be flying to the other side of the world. What would you father say!'

I stiffen and swallow the lump in my throat. She does need to know. 'Mum, about Dad…'

Jase walks in to the room on a live stream to his family back in Australia and the opportunity is lost as congratulations and explanations fly back and forth thanks to the power of technology.

What a difference twenty-four hours can make. This time yesterday I was getting ready to face the man who stole my innocence and I didn't know if Jase and I had a future together. Today he is here by my side, he knows the truth and in a few short weeks we'll be married. I don't want this moment to end. There will be issues to work through, for us all. For now, it is enough to focus on joy and gratitude.

***

Life picks up pace when we get back to Australia, there is so much to organise in six weeks. I keep pinching myself, expecting to wake from a beautiful dream, but this is my life now, these feelings are real and I am unconditionally loved beyond belief.

The early morning light streams through the bedroom window and I stretch and sigh in contentment. There is nowhere else I would rather be than here beside Jase. I glance at the man I will call my husband in a few short weeks. He catches my eye and the heat warms my cheeks.

'Come here,' he murmurs, and we make beautiful, magical love again.

Afterwards, lying in his arms, I feel safe and that nothing can harm me here.

He leans up on one elbow and drops a butterfly kiss on my nose.

'Let's go house hunting.'

'Are you serious?'

'You do want a new family home don't you?'

'Well yes of course, that would be lovely.'

'So why wait.' He reaches for his laptop from under the bed. 'What do we want? Sea view, lakeside, suburbia, city?'

There's only one answer to that. 'Beachside.'

'Good choice, my preference also.'

'Are we really talking about this? Our apartment is fine.'

'Áine, you have a son, let's make a home where he can come stay when he wants to, a safe haven where he feels he belongs. Even if you don't tell him that you're his mum, it doesn't mean that you can't have him close by.'

What have I done to deserve a man so considerate and loving? Tears stream from my eyes as I process the possibilities. For a decade I have hoped with all my heart to find a way to be a mother to my son. Jase, my hero, has made it seem possible. I smother his face with kisses. 'I love you, I love you.'

'I love you too,' he laughs. 'Now let's find this new home. Have a look at this one.'

He gives me a chance to read the property information he has up on the screen of his laptop. 'What do you think?'

'I think we should check it out.'

* * *

WOW! It looks even better up close. This was worth getting out of bed on a duvet day.

The agent is there to meet us and smiles a greeting.

We follow her into the house and I can't help an intake of breath. It's stunning. The open space, marble floors throughout, a kitchen any Masterchef would be proud of and a staircase that calls me to go to the next level, where the ocean view is breathtaking. The sea is shimmering in the sunshine.

'This is it,' I breathe.

'Yes,' agrees Jase as we stand side by side on the balcony.

'But can we afford it?'

'We can, that's all you need to worry about. If you're sure this is the house for us to build our future in together, let me do this for us.'

All I can do is laugh and nod.

He swings me around and we go to tell the agent we'll take it. Without me knowing, Jase's already organised preapproval for finance with the bank. While he talks business with the agent and they draw up an offer for the owner, I drift off into a daydream, see myself sitting in the sunroom overlooking the greenest lawn watching a mini Jase run around. Is it a vision? Whatever it is, it feels within my grasp.

'Áine.' Jase's voice calls me back to the now. 'The agent called the owner and we've got a verbal acceptance.'

'Yes? It's a yes?' I want to laugh and cry. 'This is going to be our house?'

'As soon as everything goes through, yes.'

I can't help it. With a delighted squeall throw myself into his arms.

After much laughter, the agent shakes us both by the hand. 'Congratulations to you both, I'm sure you will be very happy here.'

I'm already happier than I ever imagined I could be.

* * *

Mum is due to arrive. I have tried to talk with Cass but she isn't having any of it. I can't rock that boat too much, I need to keep things amicable so I can continue to be part of Damien's day to day life. He chooses to be with me most of the time now and I do not want that to end.

Roaming around our beautiful new home I feel so grateful for the joy that is my life. I choose to love each moment for as long as it lasts, I have come to learn not to dwell on the possibility that it all might disappear. Jase has taught me a lot about how to unconditionally love and how to be unconditionally loved, so much so that I even hope to be a major part of my son's life. The yearning to be a mother but unable to be one has shadowed my last decade. Now I feel worthy again, worthy to express my love, not supress it. I will never surrender this feeling again.

I feel like I know what it must have been like for my mother to give birth to her first child and be unable to love her as she hoped to do. For someone else to step in and claim that love and keep it all to themselves without sharing. To have to wait on the sidelines for small pockets of time when she could connect with Cass.

There's more to this story and I will get to the bottom of it. Cass doesn't treat Mum this way for no reason, there is something there! If there is any way to resolve this and build the bridge between Mum and Cass, I will find it.

***

When it is time to go to the airport to pick up Mum, I ask Cass if Damien can come with me.

Without lifting her head from the magazine she is reading, she snaps an abrupt, 'No,' and he shouts at her that she's mean and runs off to his room.

I shake my head at her. 'Cass, what is your problem with Mammy? She has only ever wanted to love you.'

She gives me an angry glare then returns to her magazine, but I can't let it go, not this time.

'It seems to me that you've been holding something in for years. Isn't it time to let it go?'

'You let it go, Áine.' She jumps up and tosses the magazine on the floor. 'If I let it out, I would never stop.'

'But whatever it is, it's not good for you to hold it in.'

'Can't you see? I have to, if I don't the toxicity will consume my life.'

'It seems like it is already.'

She drops back onto the seat and cups her face in her hands, her shoulders heaving. That's what I wanted, for her to release.

Crouching down beside her, I take her hand in mine. 'You can tell me, Cass. I'm not a child anymore, you don't have to protect me.'

She looks deep into my eyes and swipes my face with a gentle touch. 'You're not, are you? But I don't know where to start.'

'At the beginning.'

There is a long silence, then she sighs deeply. 'I was always Dad's favourite, his number one. I had this deep connection to him and he loved me so much, I could feel it. You're right, Mum never had a look in. I felt no connection to her. I think rejecting her milk when I was born meant we never had the chance to truly bond. I was an only child for years and then you came along. Mum was so happy she had someone to love. I saw how much she loved you and it was unconditional love. I began to realise that the bond between Dad and me wasn't unconditional, he would always test me and reward me when I excelled. I had to

keep that up to maintain his love. Mum loved you without you having to do anything at all.'
'But Mum loved you too, Cass.'
'If she loved me she wouldn't have stayed with Dad when he did what he did.'
'What?' A chill runs through me. 'Cass, what did he do?'
'Exactly the same as what happened to you.'
I drop back, struggling to organise my thoughts. 'But...'
'Áine, it happened to both of us. I know it's hard to get your head around. And I'm sorry I wasn't there for you.'
'It's not your fault.'
'But Mum could have stopped it, she should have left Dad years ago and none of this would have happened. There's no way she didn't know something was up. Her job was to protect us and she didn't. I'll never forgive her for that.'
'I never knew.' It comes out as a whisper.
Cass reaches for my hand. 'I didn't want you to know. Áine, I'm sorry, you've been through so much more than me. I shouldn't have run away, I should have stayed and protected you. At least I didn't have to carry the child of the man who stole my innocence. You did. Damien is here because you had the courage to bring him into the world. I don't know if I would have had that courage but I'm glad that you did. You gave me the son my heart longed to mother.'
We sit in the stillness of the secret that has just been released and there is a sense of freedom in knowing that it will no longer be hidden in the darkness, festering away inside like a soul-eating beast.
'Cass...I don't want to keep any more secrets. Secrets are hidden from fear that the truth will come with consequences that

we're not ready for but if we live a lie then we can never truly know the full potential that life has to offer us. Lies change the course of our destiny.'

'Are you saying what I think you're trying to tell me, Áine?'

'Cass, you're my sister and I love you so much and feel more connected to you than ever before. But you don't need to protect me anymore. Things are turning around for me now. I no longer need to live in the shadows of secrets. I need to be fully free from them. I want to tell Damien that I'm his mum.'

The colour drains from her cheeks and my heart sinks. All I want is to be a mother to the child I gave birth to. I know what I'm asking of her and that my gain will be her loss. I hardly dare to breathe.

When she speaks it is so softly I can barely hear her. 'Yes.'

Tears fill my eyes and my throat closes up but I manage to say, 'Thank you.'

Then something unexpected happens. Cass grabs me tight and hugs me. It is an embrace I have waited a lifetime to receive. We cling together with the tears running down our cheeks. It's as if we release the pain of the past and unite in this moment that only we can truly understand. A piece of us was once stolen and yet we have somehow turned that past negative into a future positive. I know on the deepest level that it will never be taken away again.

***

I don't know what to say to Mammy. This is a time of celebration and yet long-buried secrets are being exposed. There is so much that needs to be said but Donal will be with her so I hope we will have some time alone.

Nervousness knots my stomach when I arrive at the airport to meet them. It's as if the mother I always knew and loved has changed and I can never see her in the same light again. But I mustn't judge until I give Mammy a chance to explain things from her perspective. One thing I have learned through all of this is to never take anything for granted. Secrets can destroy people yet when they are revealed it can actually bring people together to begin a deep healing process. I have swum deep in the darkest ocean for too long. I'm ready to embrace the open waters glistening with sunlight. That knowing lightens my step as I greet Mammy and Donal and there are hugs all round.

Once the luggage has been collected and we're all in the car, Donal pops in his ear buds and zonks in the back seat. It's the perfect opportunity for me to raise the issues with Mammy that have been running through my mind without relief ever since I went to Ireland.

I can't hold back any longer. 'Mammy, I need to ask you something important.'

'Yes, of course, love,' she says. 'Anything.'

'Why did you not stop Dad from grooming us for that horrid man?'

A sideways glance shows the blood has drained from her face and she is clenching the handbag on her lap so tightly her knuckles are white. She quickly checks the back seat to make sure Donal is asleep.

'You want the truth.'

'Yes, Mammy, no more lies.'

'It is time you knew.'

She takes a deep breath. I know how hard this will be for her, so I reach over to briefly touch her cheek and find it is wet with silent tears. Her voice falters when she begins to speak but she quickly gets it under control.

'I always knew something was amiss. Your father was so attentive to me and to you girls but there was something I couldn't put my finger on. You see he went to great lengths to shield me from the outside world and I only really knew what he shared with me. It's hard to believe that all those years I didn't know what was happening, but love, I promise I didn't. If I had, I would have protected you and your sister. It wasn't until I followed your dad to the so-called office one morning that it all fell into place for me and I knew he had poisoned the childhood of my beautiful girls. I felt sick, my whole married life flashed before my eyes. I had given up everything for this man so that we could build a beautiful family together and he was not the man I'd believed him to be. I thought he was a doting dad who loved to spend time with you girls and watch you grow. When I think of all the times I wasn't around…it makes me sick…'

A sob shudders through her and I pull over to the side of the road so I can hug her and tell her I love her and that everything will be all right.

She pulls a bunch of tissues from the box I have in the car and mops at her eyes. 'I should've known, love, I really should have. Looking back I can see all the signs but at the time I didn't. Not until I saw him behaving with Donal in a way that wasn't normal for a father. I knew then. And he knew that I knew. He saw it in my eyes and…' She stops and stares through the windscreen.

'And what, Mammy?' The tension in the car is almost palpable and I realise I am shaking.

'He knew I would take action and so he tried to silence me. But my fury at what he did to you three, my precious children, made my strength more powerful than his and while we were struggling, he went into cardiac arrest. So…I killed him.'

'No, you said it was his heart.'

'Yes, and when I realised what was happening, I couldn't help myself. I held a pillow over his face and made sure that he would never breathe life into his evil body again.'

I am stunned. I don't know what to say, what to feel. There is relief that she didn't know, wasn't part of the conspiracy for abuse. For I do believe her. But should I be glad that my mother killed my father? Was what she did right? These are questions I may never answer. What I do know is that I forgive her for not knowing and I tell her so. I hope it will lighten the burden of guilt she carries.

As I start the car and pull back into traffic, Mammy says, 'I need to tell Cass. She needs to know too.'

'She already does, she heard the whole thing. I phoned her when we got into the car.' I put it on speaker.

'Hi, Mum,' Cass blubbers.

'Oh, my darling Cassandra, it's you. You heard? Everything?'

'Yes, Mum.'

Tears and laughter fill the car.

Donal begins to stir. 'Are we there yet?'

Mammy and I laugh. 'No, Donal love, go back to sleep.'

'Mammy, why don't you drop by here on your way to Áine's house,' suggests Cass. 'I'm sure Mick and Damien would love to meet you.'

The joy in Mammy's voice is impossible to miss. 'Really?'
'Yes, really.'
Mammy looks to me. 'Can we?'
"We're on our way, Cass,' I say and disconnect the call.
For the next thirty minutes we sit in silence. Mammy can't stop smiling and her happiness is infectious.
'I just realised something,' she says as we turn the corner into the street where Cass lives. 'My greatest wish is about to come true. I have never had all three of my children in one place with me ever. I have wished for this for so long.'
'And Mammy, guess what?'
'I don't know if my heart can take any more surprises, love.'
'Cass says that she is okay for me to tell Damien that I am his mum.'
'Oh my sweet darling girl. It is the dream.'
'It truly is. Ever since Jase asked me to marry him something has shifted my life onto a whole new spectrum. At first it felt like I was spiralling out of control but in fact it was all just swirling together. I feel like pinching myself.'
'It's all the secrets, love, they're toxic and no good for anyone. It is better when everything is out in the open because it is from that point that we can make choices based on the principle of truth.'
'Wise words, Mammy.'
Cass is sitting on a bench in the garden waiting for us when we arrive. She runs to the car and greets Mam with the biggest hug. Tears flow from all of us as years of toxicity wash away. Donal stands back at first, not quite sure why we are all being so emotional, then he shrugs and joins the group embraces. There is still much he doesn't know yet. Later, we will tell him what we

now know. For the moment I am filled with gratitude that we are all together and at last Mammy is free to enjoy her family without the burdens of the past. She has an abundance of love to give and we now feel worthy and ready to receive it.

I turn around and there is Damien looking at me. This is the moment, I can feel it surge through me.
'Damien, can I chat to you for a moment?'
'Yeah sure' he seems a bit snappy.
'Is something wrong?'
'Why didn't you ever tell me? I should have known it feels so strange to know that you're my real mum.'
Cass has told him already and I am at peace with that. I reach out to hug him and am met with a slight resistance, but he soon surrenders to my embrace.
'I have always loved you as my son, I was just very young.'
'I know.' He buries his head into my shoulders and I finally hug my son.'
Then the word I yearned a decade to hear.
'Mum.'
Tears flow from my eyes and my heart is full. 'Yes son.'
'Does this mean that I can come live with you and Jase in the cool house.'
I laugh 'Of course it does.'
We hug and I don't want to let go. At the side of my eye I see Cass peek out the window, she smiles at me and I gesture *thank you*.

***

It's the day of the wedding. A lot has happened since mammy arrived last week. But most of all we have connected, we have laughed and we have been a family. Jase is such a supportive man, he has gone out of his way for my family and was there to welcome Damien into our home, he will be a great dad. Something like that can be huge for a young man but he has taken it in his stride. Perhaps because I have always been there, doing things for him and caring for him as he grew, it wasn't so much of a shock. Cass has stepped back into the aunty role with love. It has given her and Mick more time to focus on each other and their relationship. Something magical has happened with them.

I look at myself in the mirror, every bit the bride I hoped I would be. I've chosen a hand-embroidered halter-neck satin gown, the dress I have always dreamed of wearing on my special day.
Cass and Mammy travel with me to the beachside location we have chosen for our special day. I know they are so proud of me and are happy that I have found the love I deserve.
The air is warm and inviting as we emerge from the car. On the beach our family and friends are gathered and the man I love stands waiting at the top of the aisle between the seats.
The music begins and I take the first steps towards him with Damien by my side. I can't help but think briefly that if my father had been a loving parent and not the monster he was, it would be he who would give me away today and not my son. But I am present in this moment, I know that everything is exactly as it should be. The music dictates every step we take and even though I want to run down the sandy aisle into the arms of the

man I love, it is wonderful to see the smiling faces of the people who mean so much to us.

I am soon standing at the exact point on the beach where we stood at six months ago when I didn't know if the secrets of my past would destroy any future I had with Jase. I was trapped in an internal prison that I knew I had to find the courage to break out from. I did, I am here facing the man I love, surrounded by all of our loved ones, ready to embrace a future together as one. This is the life I choose.

'Do you, Jase Norman Greaves take Áine Angela O'Brien to be your lawfully wedded wife?' asks the celebrant.

'I do.' His voice is strong and clear.

The love beaming from this man's eyes warms every cell in my body. I know our growing child will feel this love as much as I do.

'Do you, Áine Angela O'Brien take Jase Norman Greaves to be your lawfully married husband?'

'I do.' I have never felt as certain about anything in my life.

'Congratulations, you are now man and wife. You may kiss the bride.'

Not a second is lost before Jase kisses me so lovingly and our friends and family cheer with delight.

The sun begins to set and we move to the beachside café where Jase first proposed for our reception. There is a wonderful mood of celebration throughout the evening as the meal is followed by speeches both heartfelt and hilarious and the disco dancing kicks off. Jase has had a few drinks and is showing the kids some breakdance moves when Cass slips up beside me.

'He's such a good guy, Áine.'

'I know.'

'I'm so glad you worked things out with each other.'

'So am I. And Cass…I'm pregnant!'

'I am too,' she confides. 'I wasn't going to tell you till after the wedding because this is your special day.'

I can't help a squeal of delight. 'It's wonderful news. We're pregnant together! I couldn't be more pleased. Have you told Mick yet?'

'No, have you told Jase?'

'I was going to tell him tonight.'

'Oh bugger this,' she laughs. 'Follow me.'

Cass leads me across the room. She whispers something into the ear of the DJ and he calls Mick and Jase to the dance floor. Also, Mammy and Damien.

Cass takes the microphone. 'Hello, everyone, we have something to share and as this has been the most perfect day ever for our family, we thought…' She grabs my hand and beams out at the gathering. '…we thought that you would like to also celebrate the news that we are both pregnant.'

Cheers fill the room. Jase and Mick give each other a high five and then gently swing us around the dance floor in celebration. Mammy and Damien hug each other.

The future is bright, for the secrets of our past have been revealed and healing has begun. We will swim the oceans of life in open sea without any darkness shadowing us.

About the Author

Karen Weaver is an author of books across many genres.

Beginning her writing journey at adoptamum.com. in 2010, filled to the brim with creativness after having her 4th child she began writing short pieces of interest, this soon grew into featured articles and then her first novel The Visitor was born through the belief and support she received from this community.

She went on to write and publish The Wish Giver in 2012 whilst also writing articles and founding her first publishing company, Serenity Press.

Karen knows that it is because she was given the opportunity to discover her natural writing ability through the freedom of exploration that she has successfully incorporated writing into her life. Now a mother of 6 and is currently writing her 4th novel in the series 'The Shadow Keeper'.

Now the author of 30 books, including #1 bestseller Mindful Magic, Karen will continue to write and share her stories with readers of all interests.

You can find out more about Karen at
www.karenweaverauthor.com
https://www.facebook.com/KarenWeaverAuthor/
hhtps://www.instagram.com/karenweaverauthor

More Books by Karen Include:

Fiction
The Enlightenment Series:
The Visitor
The Wish Giver
The Memory Taker

Novelettes
Forbidden Love
Beached
Lavender Dreams

Non-Fiction
Mindful Magic
The Power of Knowing
Everything Publishing
Writing the Dream
Magical Moments

Children's books
Alphabet Job Buddies
Minky Monkey meets series
One Sunny Day
Roly Poly Rainbow Princess
Bumble Bee Rock Around the Clock
Australian Animal Walkabout
Irish Dancing Girl

Lightning Source UK Ltd.
Milton Keynes UK
UKHW011042150121
377095UK00001B/49